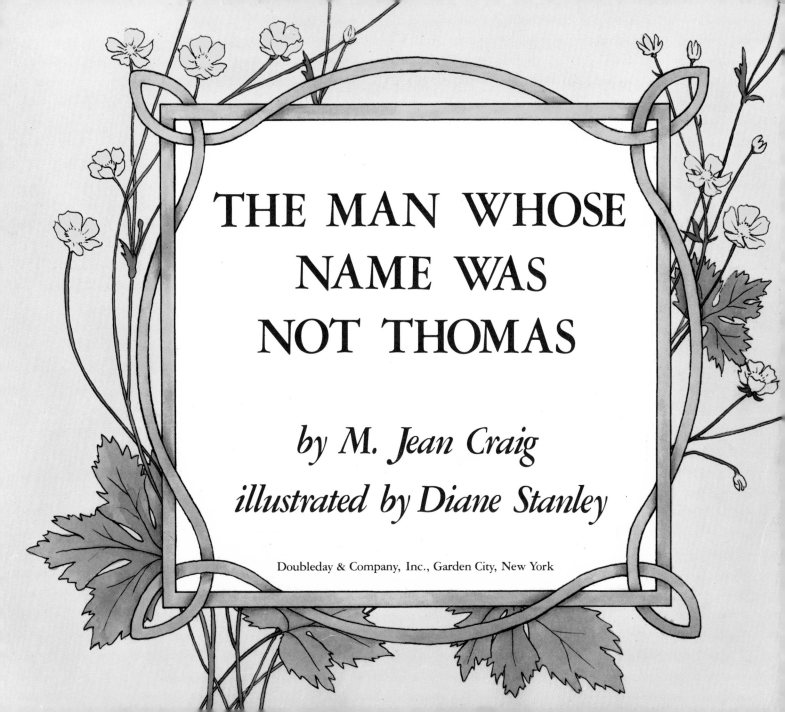

THE MAN WHOSE NAME WAS NOT THOMAS

by M. Jean Craig

illustrated by Diane Stanley

Doubleday & Company, Inc., Garden City, New York

ISBN: 0-385-15064-4 Trade
0-385-15065-2 Prebound
Library of Congress Catalog Card Number 78-22626
Text copyright © 1981 by M. Jean Craig
Illustrations copyright © 1981 by Diane Stanley
Printed in the United States of America
First Edition

For Neill S. Barber with my love
M. J. C.

For Carl, who is special
D. S.

nce, a good many years ago, there was a man whose name was not Thomas. His name was not Richard, either. His name was not Bruce or Victor or Henry. His name was not Leo or Simon or Charles. In fact, his name was not even John. No, his name was something else.

The man whose name was not Thomas, or Richard either, had to earn a living, just as most men do. He was not a blacksmith or a carpenter. He did not weave cloth or mend shoes. He was not a farmer or a bricklayer or a fisherman. He was something else.

He lived in a small corner next to the big oven in the room behind his shop. His oven was not made of tin or glass or leather or paper. It was made of something else.

The man whose name was not Thomas (or Bruce or Victor) did not bake bread in his big oven. He did not bake pies or cookies. And he never even thought of baking potatoes or biscuits or squash. No, he baked something else.

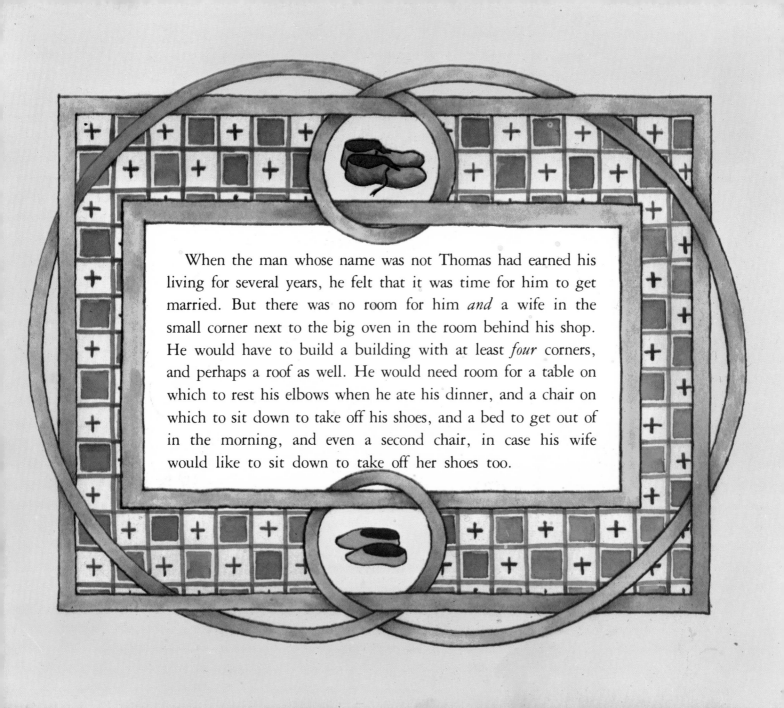

When the man whose name was not Thomas had earned his living for several years, he felt that it was time for him to get married. But there was no room for him *and* a wife in the small corner next to the big oven in the room behind his shop. He would have to build a building with at least *four* corners, and perhaps a roof as well. He would need room for a table on which to rest his elbows when he ate his dinner, and a chair on which to sit down to take off his shoes, and a bed to get out of in the morning, and even a second chair, in case his wife would like to sit down to take off her shoes too.

What sort of building should he build? The man whose name was not Thomas thought long and hard, and at last he decided. He would not build a chicken coop. He would not build a tower or a barn. He would not build a watermill or a castle or a jail.

No, indeed, he would not; he decided that he would build something else.

And he did. He did not build it of buttons. He did not build it of sand. He did not build it of corncobs or ribbons or feathers or forks. No, the man whose name was not Thomas, or Henry or Leo, built it tight and built it well because he built it of something else.

Now that there was a place to put a table and a chair and a bed and another chair, all that he had to do was find a wife.

He knew just what sort of wife he wanted. He did not want a wife with green hair or orange eyes or an extra nose growing out of her chin. He did not want a wife as fat as a barrel of oil or as thin as a bundle of sticks. He did not want a wife who hated rainbows and puppy-dogs, or who never, never laughed out loud. And he certainly did not want a wife who would be hard to love.

No, the man whose name was not Thomas did not want a wife like any of these wives. He wanted someone else. And he knew where to find her, too, for she lived just down the lane.

Now, a man who is about to go courting must look clean and bright and tidy, so the man whose name was not Thomas, or Simon or Charles, dressed very carefully. He did not put on a dirty apron or a sweater with a hole in the elbow. He did not put on a torn jacket with three buttons missing. No, he wore something else, and he looked very clean and very bright and very tidy indeed when he set off down the lane to do his courting.

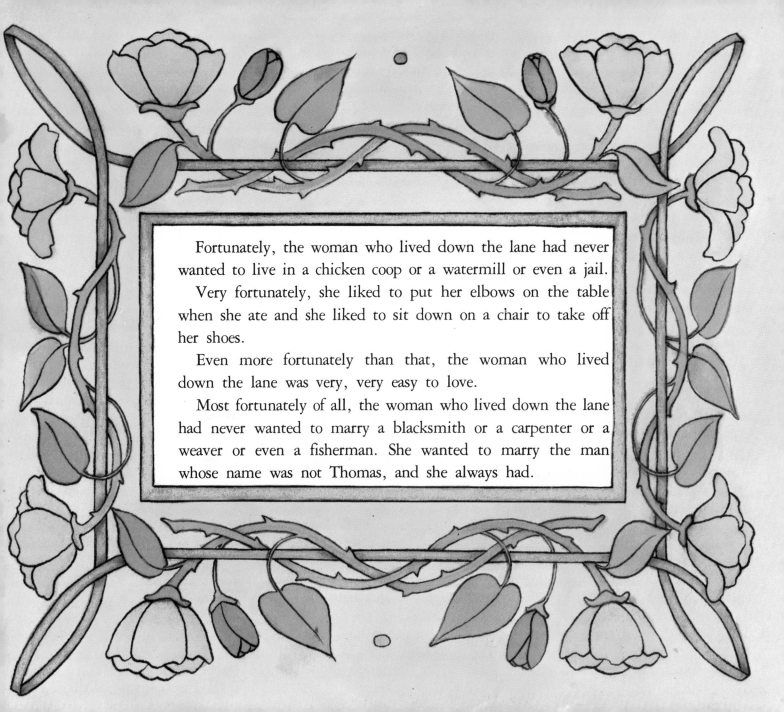

Fortunately, the woman who lived down the lane had never wanted to live in a chicken coop or a watermill or even a jail.

Very fortunately, she liked to put her elbows on the table when she ate and she liked to sit down on a chair to take off her shoes.

Even more fortunately than that, the woman who lived down the lane was very, very easy to love.

Most fortunately of all, the woman who lived down the lane had never wanted to marry a blacksmith or a carpenter or a weaver or even a fisherman. She wanted to marry the man whose name was not Thomas, and she always had.

MONDAY

So when the man whose name was not Thomas asked her to marry him, she said that she would, a week from tomorrow. A week from tomorrow was not Monday or Friday or Wednesday. A week from tomorrow was not Saturday or Tuesday. It was not Thursday, either, but something else. It was a very good day to get married.

TVESDAY

The man whose name was not Thomas (or even John) rushed home to get ready for the wedding. After all, a man who is not a shoemaker or a farmer or a bricklayer has a special job to do any time a wedding is planned.

He does not have to sweep the church. He does not have to practice on his fiddle. He does not have to pick flowers for the altar. But he does have to do something else.

So the man whose name was not Thomas *did* something else, and did it just beautifully, and finished doing it just in time for the wedding.

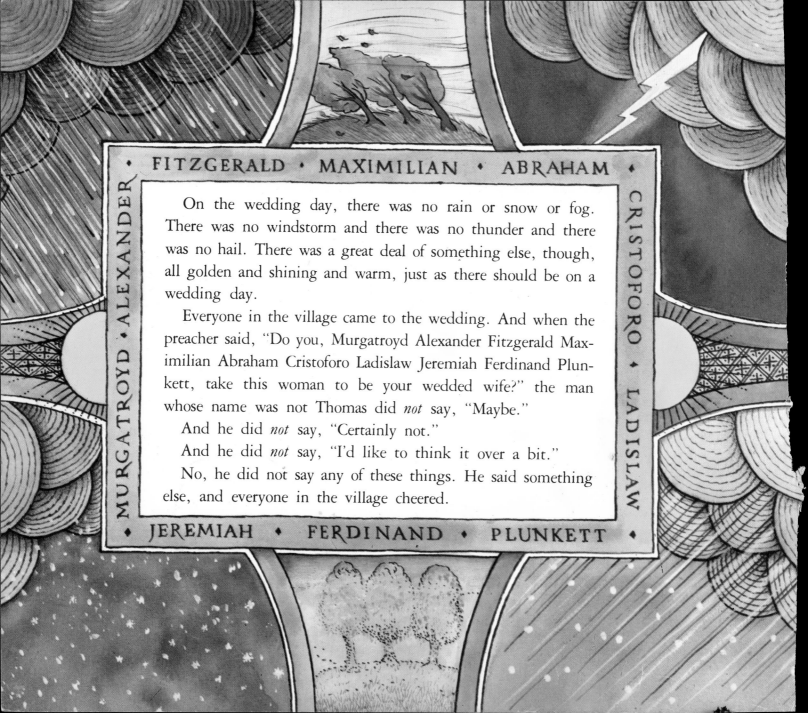

FITZGERALD · MAXIMILIAN · ABRAHAM

MURGATROYD · ALEXANDER

CRISTOFORO · LADISLAW

On the wedding day, there was no rain or snow or fog. There was no windstorm and there was no thunder and there was no hail. There was a great deal of something else, though, all golden and shining and warm, just as there should be on a wedding day.

Everyone in the village came to the wedding. And when the preacher said, "Do you, Murgatroyd Alexander Fitzgerald Maximilian Abraham Cristoforo Ladislaw Jeremiah Ferdinand Plunkett, take this woman to be your wedded wife?" the man whose name was not Thomas did *not* say, "Maybe."

And he did *not* say, "Certainly not."

And he did *not* say, "I'd like to think it over a bit."

No, he did not say any of these things. He said something else, and everyone in the village cheered.

JEREMIAH · FERDINAND · PLUNKETT

And so the man whose name was not Thomas, or any number of other fine names, was married, and he and his wife went to live where there were four corners and a roof and enough room for a table and a bed and a chair and another chair, and they are living there together still.

They are not lonely. They are not sad.

They are not angry or poor or sick or frightened.

No, not in the least.

They are something else.

About the Author

M. Jean Craig became interested in writing for children when she began reading to her two young daughters. She has since written more than twenty books for children, both fiction and nonfiction. Ms. Craig now lives in an old Long Island farmhouse on the edge of a meadow, five minutes from half a dozen different bay beaches, and ten minutes from the ocean. This is her second book for Doubleday; her first was *The Donkey Prince*. Other books by Ms. Craig include *Dinosaurs and More Dinosaurs*, *Little Monsters*, and *Questions and Answers About Weather*.

About the Illustrator

Diane Stanley was born in Abilene, Texas. After studying art in Edinburgh, Scotland, and at Johns Hopkins University School of Medicine, Ms. Stanley received her M.A. in medical and biological illustration. After her two daughters were born, she became interested in children's literature and has since worked in a publishing company as art director for the children's book department and has illustrated several books of her own, some under the name of Diane Stanley Zuromskis. THE MAN WHOSE NAME WAS NOT THOMAS is her first book for Doubleday.